Ghost Cat
and Other
Spooky
Tales

by James Preller

SCHOLASTIC INC.

New York   Toronto   London   Auckland   Sydney

Mexico City   New Delhi   Hong Kong   Buenos Aires

In memory of the real, true Blue

No part of this publication may be reproduced, stored in a retrieval system, or transmitted in any form or by any means, electronic, mechanical, photocopying, recording, or otherwise, without written permission of the publisher. For information regarding permission, write to Scholastic Inc., Attention: Permissions Department, 557 Broadway, New York, NY 10012.

ISBN-13: 978-0-439-79398-8
ISBN-10: 0-439-79398-X

Text copyright © 2006 by James Preller.
Illustrations copyright © 2006 by Scholastic Inc.
SCHOLASTIC, LITTLE APPLE, and associated logos are
trademarks and/or registered trademarks of Scholastic Inc.

12 11 10 9 8 7 6   17 18 19 20

Printed in the U.S.A.   40

First printing, February 2006

Contents

GHOST CAT

"Aaaaaaccck!" Mother screamed.

Her scream threaded down the stairs, through the hall, and into the playroom. Maggie and Gavin dropped their toys. They bounded upstairs. "What's wrong?" the children called.

Mother stood at the doorway to her bedroom. She pointed to a dead mouse on the rug. "Blue left us another present," she grumbled.

Maggie and Gavin stepped forward. Maggie bent down, fascinated. On all fours, she brought her nose close to the dead animal.

"Get away. Don't touch it," Mother scolded. "I'll be right back with a dustpan."

The mouse was gray and sleek. Its four little pink paws lay outstretched, as if it were about to run away. Its eyes stared straight ahead. Cold and blank like marbles. Its mouth was open slightly to show two small, sharp teeth.

"Cool," Maggie purred.

"Blue got another," Gavin noted. "That's his second mouse this week." He saw the dried red scab behind the

creature's neck. In every other way, the body was unharmed. Even beautiful, in a way, for a gray mouse.

Soon Mother came up, brushed the children aside, and swept up the dead rodent. Old Blue, the cat, came sashaying down the hallway. Chin up, triumphant, paws stepping lightly.

"Blue is proud of herself," Mother said as she dropped the body into a brown garbage bag. "Look at her. She thinks she's the cat's meow."

Maggie lifted old Blue in her arms. The cat gave herself completely, relaxed and comfortable, into the young girl's grip. She purred and licked herself on the belly.

Gavin stood beside his mother. "Dad says it's good that Blue kills mice," he said. "He says it's her job. Blue scares the other mice away to the Jaffe-Kleins' house next door."

Mother smiled. "Yes, I suppose it's better to have a dead mouse than a live one. But I still wish Blue wouldn't leave them around the house like little presents. I almost stepped on this one."

"Gross," Maggie said.

"You're telling me," Mother agreed.

Almost overnight, something about old Blue changed. One day, for no reason at all, she lay resting by a wall vent in Gavin's room. Warm air flowed over her blue-gray coat. She didn't come down for breakfast. Not even for a bowl of milk.

"Something's wrong," Mother fretted. "This isn't like Blue."

True, the cat was almost fourteen

years old. Her fur, once so soft and clean, looked scruffy. The children gathered around. Blue's head swiveled stiffly, heavily. She put her head on the rug. Too tired to move. Blue watched them with her eyes until they closed to a sliver, a thin slant. Shut.

Later the children brought up a woolen blanket and a bowl of water. Still, Blue did not move. She did not drink.

Father took old Blue to the vet first thing the following morning. He carried her in a blanket, driving with the cat on his lap. Old Blue, the fearless mouse-killer, did not move to protest.

"The doctor took some tests," Father told the family after dinner. "She's suffering from kidney failure. That means her body isn't working properly.

Old Blue is dying. It's like she has poison in her blood, but there's no way to get rid of it. She's too sick."

Gavin, Maggie, and Mother sat in silence. "Dr. Neilly says I should bring her in tomorrow. He'll give her a shot — it will not hurt — and old Blue will go to sleep."

". . . And she won't ever wake up," Maggie, the youngest, said.

"That's right," Father replied. "Old Blue will never wake up."

One by one, they rose from their seats. They climbed the stairs. The family quietly walked into Gavin's room. And they sat with old Blue for a long, long time. Maggie held her. And Gavin held her. And Mother remembered the day she found Blue, just a kitten, many years before. "She was the cutest thing I'd ever seen," Mother said. They all laughed, remembering happy times.

Until, at last, it was time to turn out the light.

That's when strange things started to happen.

Blue had been "gone" for three days. The house seemed empty without her. Gavin or Maggie would walk into a room and expect to see her curled up on the couch, lounging in a slant of sunlight. But Blue wasn't there. All the same, it was almost like she was there. Like an echo.

"I heard her last night," Maggie confessed to Gavin. The boy looked into his sister's eyes. He put down his Star Wars lightsaber.

"She was meowing," Maggie told him.

"It couldn't be," Gavin replied. "Blue is gone."

"No," Maggie said solemnly. "She's still here."

"Do you believe in ghosts?" Gavin asked Father.

"Ghosts?" He looked at his son, who was absently working his way through a bowl of Rice Krispies. "Well, no. At least I don't think so. How about you?"

"I don't think so, either," Gavin repeated. The boy tended to agree with his father about most things.

"I do," Maggie answered. Her eyes were wide. She whispered, "Ghosts are real."

"Oh, sweetheart," Father said, "don't be silly. There are no such things as ghosts."

"There are," Maggie insisted. And she said it in such a way, with such utter confidence, that it was impossible not to believe her. A zipper of fear crawled down Father's spine.

Something brushed against Gavin's dreams as he slept. It was warm and ticklish, like the tail of a cat.

His eyes shot open.

The light scamper of feet padded down the hallway.

Blue, he thought.

And he turned, rolling over, returning to the place where boys dream.

Maggie found it the next morning.

A dead mouse.

In the same spot as the others, near Mother's bedroom door.

Again the children gathered around.

"Look!" Gavin pointed. There was a scab of blood on the back of the neck.

Maggie reached out a finger. She touched the dead creature.

"Still warm," she said.

Gavin nodded.

Together, they shared one thought: *Blue*.

There was a family meeting that night.

"I hear her crying every night," Maggie said.

"I've laid down on my pillow," Gavin told them, "and it was warm, like Blue had been sleeping there."

Then Father looked to Mother.

"I've heard it, too," she confessed. "A mewing at night."

"I think that Blue is sad," Maggie said.

The father looked into his daughter's slate-gray eyes. He looked into his son's eyes, which perfectly mirrored his own. Then Father took a deep breath. "I've read books about this sort of thing."

The children leaned closer. This, they wanted to hear.

"They say that sometimes, after a person or an animal dies, that maybe his or her spirit will stay around for a little while."

"Like a ghost," Maggie murmured.

"People believe the reason for this," Father explained, "is because there is *something* unfinished."

"Something unfinished?" Mother echoed.

12

"Yes, a job or something. A task of some kind," Father mused.

The family sat in silence. "The mice," Gavin suggested. "You used to say that was Blue's job. Chasing the mice away."

Maggie nodded. "Blue is sad about the mice," she confirmed. "She is worried about us."

"Then we have to help Blue stop worrying," Father announced. "She was a wonderful cat. We all loved her. Old Blue deserves to rest."

And so it was decided. Somebody else would have to kill the mice from now on.

The next Saturday, Mother came home carrying two kittens. Black ones, a brother and a sister. They were nine weeks old and you could barely tell them apart. So one wore a red collar. The other wore a yellow collar.

Maggie held one.

Gavin held the other.

And the ghost of Blue was never seen or heard ever again. Her job, at last, was finished.

THE CREATURE IN THE CLOSET

Angelina Dreyfuss, age eleven, was in love.

In love with her very own self.

Of course, when most people look into a mirror, we find something wrong. Sure, we might like the overall effect.

15

A nice face, a good face. But there are always flaws. Certain details are not quite right. We might not love the color of our eyes (too brown), or the size of our teeth (too small), or the unsightly shape of our nose (too crooked).

This only makes perfect sense. Because, after all, no one is perfect.

Except for Angelina. She *adored* gazing in mirrors. And every time that Angelina saw her reflection, she thought, *Just perfect.*

In truth, Angelina was not far from wrong. She *was* beautiful, stunningly so, and in every way. Her eyes were almond-shaped, set into her skull like flawless gems. Her nose was ladylike and dainty, but not *too* dainty. Her lips were full and red. Her hair was a lavish brunette.

Angelina admired herself for hours at a time. No mirror eluded her loving gaze. She would stop before store windows — not to look inside, but to see herself reflected back in the glass. Smiling, she would secretly wave to herself, as if greeting a best friend. During meals, Angelina would even pause while lifting a spoon, just to see her face gazing back. *Just perfect*, she'd think.

Of course, the world is a big place. Angelina could not possibly hang mirrors everywhere. It was not practical. So she carried with her at all times a pink purse. Among other items, it contained a small ebony hand mirror. So that no matter where she was, or what she was doing, a mirror would never be far from Angelina's reach.

Is such a thing vanity? Too much

pride? Too much ego? Is it wrong to love oneself so very, very much?

Yet would not a rainbow step back to admire itself, if only it could? Does not an eagle, soaring above the mountain cliffs, think, *Oh, what a wonderful thing am I?*

Now, dear reader, we are sure you know what to expect next in our little tale. The nasty girl, beautiful though she may be, will learn a lesson about the perils of vanity. And even perhaps, in a book such as this, be turned into a newt or some other slithering, slathering creature!

Alas, not so.

Read on, please, and you'll see what we mean.

Before bed each night, Angelina always brushed her hair with one

hundred strokes, fifty on each side. She would look into a mirror and note with satisfaction the perfectness of her tidy white teeth. But on this particular night, a frightful groan interrupted her fancy.

"*Wooooooooh,*" it moaned, sending a chill down Angelina's lovely spine. Whatever could that be?

"*Owwwwwww.*"

The noise seemed to be coming from her closet.

Oh, dear.

Of course, it could only mean one thing — especially in a book such as this. Yes, the noise came from the horrible mouth of a horrible creature. A monster, in fact. And one who liked to EAT small children for breakfast, lunch, and dinner!

In the next moment, a loud rapping

came from the closet. *Bang, bang, bang.* The door splintered with each blow. Finally, *WHAM!*, down it crashed. And a hideous monster leaped out of the closet!

It was six feet tall and dressed in rags. Green skin, one bloodshot eye, with sharp teeth and claws. Drool slipped from its swollen lips.

Angelina sighed. She carefully set down her ebony hand mirror on her lap. "What is it?" She scowled.

"*Grrroargh!*" the creature roared. "I have come to eat you up!"

Thought Angelina: *How very inconvenient.* She was hardly halfway done with her brushing! But still, she noted, the creature did look fierce. And its teeth did look frightfully sharp. Angelina shook her head, "No, I'm afraid that I can't let you do that. I do not wish to be eaten. I have major plans for the weekend."

What?! The creature was taken aback. This was not the usual response. Children were supposed to scream, beg for mercy, and jabber terribly. It was half the fun. The creature howled again, even louder than before. "I will MUNCH on your BONES!"

"Would you not prefer a cookie?" Angelina offered, holding a small plate of jelly-filled treats.

The creature howled in disgust. It raised its pitiful claws and stepped closer to poor Angelina.

Oh, my. This pesky beast really does wish to eat me, Angelina decided. Well, she'd have to do something about that.

"Very well," the young girl replied. "I hate to do this, but I have a monstrous friend of my own. Bigger and more horrible than even you!" she cried.

Once again, the creature paused. It glanced around the room. It saw only pink curtains, dolls neatly placed on a shelf, fluffy pillows, and Angelina herself — who looked quite tasty.

"There's no one here but you," the vile creature howled, "and you won't be here for long!"

Closer it stepped, closer and closer. It opened its horrible mouth (which, frankly, smelled of cabbage) wider and wider.

At the last possible moment, Angelina grabbed her mirror and thrust it into the face of the monster. "Look!" she screamed. "My friend is here! Now YOU are the one who will be EATEN!"

The monster, who did not share

Angelina's fondness for mirrors, had never before seen such a terrible sight. For toward it came a green-skinned creature with sharp teeth and claws. It had only one eye and it drooled hungrily.

"ACK!" it cried. In that same instant, the monster opened a window, leaped out of the house, and ran for its life in fright.

Angelina, who was not only vain but pretty clever, too, smiled to herself. "What a beast," she commented. And once again she turned the mirror to herself, while she commenced brushing her hair.

THE HOUSE THAT SCREAMED

Nick paused at the top of the stairs. He checked on the baby. She was in the crib. Fast asleep. His parents were outside. No one else was home. And yet there was someone else — or some*thing* else — alive in the house.

Ever since his family moved to this new house, just two weeks ago, Nick had heard noises. The groaning of floorboards. The hissing of old radiators. And, he thought, muffled voices. Whispers. A moaning that made him reach for the light switch or turn up the radio. Loud.

The voices were talking to him. Nick was sure of it. But he didn't understand the words. What were the voices trying to say? Who else lived in this house? And who had lived here before?

WHAM!

A door slammed shut.

"Mom . . . ?"

"Dad . . . ?"

No answer. Nick was alone. Just him, the sleeping baby, and the house.

*　　*　　*

Nick Golub had, upon his head, an unlikely pile of tightly coiled black hair. The problem was, it grew quickly and unevenly. If you were to glance at the tall, frail, dark-featured boy, you would get the uneasy sense he was toppling over. Of course, he was not. No, it was that blasted hair that made him look . . . *unbalanced*.

Nick attempted a variety of goopy gels. They were of no use. Even hats refused to perch upon that wild head of hair. Finally Nick threw up his hands in exasperation. "Forget it," he vowed before the bathroom mirror, "I surrender."

So he tossed a comb, two brushes, and one tube of Stay Put styling gel into the trash. Nick Golub had not attempted to train his hair since. It was free to be whatever it wished to be.

And today it wished to resemble a windswept tumbleweed.

After dinner, Nick sat alone in the kitchen, building a Lego robot. It was one of his favorite activities, just following the directions step-by-step until the job was done. His mother was putting the baby to bed. His father was installing new tile in the downstairs bathroom.

Whirrrrr.

Nick turned to look at the counter. He expected to see his mother standing there. She was not. The kitchen was empty.

But the blender was on.

Whirrrrrnnn, it sounded. Then slower, a little bit different this time: *Wirrrrrnnning*.

Nick listened closer. It wasn't just that the blender was suddenly on — which was enough to worry about — but that it sounded like the blender was trying to speak.

Whirrrrnnning . . . wirrrning . . . wirning.

Warning, thought Nick.

He stood to snap the blender off. But it was already in the OFF position. He yanked the cord out of the electrical socket, and the sound died with it.

That night Nick slept with the radio on.

"Probably a power surge," his father gruffly explained the next day. His hand fumbled for a tool.

From where Nick stood, he could see only his father's feet, legs, and torso. His head was underneath the bathroom sink, obscured by the countertop.

"But, Dad," Nick said. "You don't seem to understand. The blender turned on all by itself."

"*Ouch!*" his father muttered angrily (he had scraped a knuckle against a pipe). "Nick, buddy," his father said, growing irritated. "I've got a leaky bathroom sink. I'm redoing all the rooms, one by one. I'm looking at a solid year's worth of what your mother would call 'little projects.' This is not a good time for me to —"

"It's *never* a good time," Nick retorted.

Uh-oh. That came out a little harsh.

Nick's father painfully climbed out from beneath the sink. He set aside his tools and wiped his hands on a rag. He looked at his only son.

"Nick, let me try to explain this to you one more time," his father said. "We are not rich people. This house is what real estate agents call 'a fixer-upper.' You know what that means? It's a dump. I've got a list of jobs coming out the wazoo. Plus, working the night shift at the correctional facility is no walk in the park. I work *hard*."

Nick nodded. "I know, Dad. I'm sorry, it's just that the blender . . ."

His father glanced briefly toward the ceiling. He ran his fingers through his thick mustache and sighed. "This is a very old house," he said slowly. "Old plumbing, old pipes, old wires. I've got to bring everything up to code, slowly but surely. But until then, we might have some power surges and blown fuses. That's what happens in old houses."

"Okay, Dad," Nick said. "I guess it's nothing."

"That's right," his father replied, once again crawling under the sink. "It's probably nothing."

In school that day, Nick learned something new.

It wasn't about math or science. It was about his new home.

"You moved into the Thompson place," Ed Gibson remarked as they ate lunch in the cafeteria.

Nick saw Ed grin at Sinjay, who sat across from him. Sinjay stifled a laugh.

"What's so funny?" Nick asked.

Ed set his meaty hands on the table.

He was a thick, powerful, dark-skinned boy. "You haven't seen any ghosts, have you?" he asked.

Nick's jaw must have dropped open. But he didn't answer. He knew enough not to answer a question like that. Not in a new school. Not when he was just starting to make friends. "Why?" he asked.

Sinjay chimed in, "He's just messing with you, Nick. Isn't that right?"

"Right, just fooling around," Ed said with a smile. But then he leaned forward and looked Nick in the eye. "The old guy who owned that place fell down the basement stairs one night and died," he said. "Nobody knows how it happened. Or even what he was doing down there. They just found him a couple of days later, dead as a doornail. What I wonder is: Did he jump? Or was he pushed?"

Nick swallowed hard. He looked at Sinjay. "For real?" he asked.

Sinjay nodded solemnly. "It's been six months since anybody lived there," he said. "Now I guess you know why your parents got such a good price."

Nick's mother wiped down the kitchen table, sponging the crumbs into her hand. She went to the garbage can, lifted the lid, and . . . suddenly stopped. She looked closely. "How did this get in here?"

She reached inside and lifted out the blender.

"Nick?" she asked. "Do you know anything about this?"

But Nick didn't answer. He was too busy drawing.

It was a picture of a house.
It was on fire.

The basement was creepy. It was cold and clammy. Dark and smelly. There was really no reason for Nick to go down there. His parents said that one day they were going to finish it. That meant they'd lay down a cement floor, put up some walls, a tile ceiling, and turn it into a playroom for Nick and his baby sister. But not yet. For now, it felt like a musty tomb.

Nick was alone, watching television in the living room. His dad was napping upstairs, catching up from the night shift. Mom and the baby were out shopping. They'd be home soon.

That's when the banging started.

Wham. A pause. *Wham.* Silence. *Wham, wham, wham.*

Nick hit the MUTE button. The noise was coming from the basement. He walked to the top of the old wooden stairs and looked down. Into the darkness.

Wham . . . wham . . . wham.

The oil burner, Nick thought. He wondered if he should wake his father. *Not a good idea,* he decided.

Nick walked down one step, then another. His hand felt for the railing. It was dark, but fractured sunlight sifted in through two small, dirty windows near the top of one wall. He could see well enough, Nick decided. Besides, there was a light down here somewhere.

WHAM!

Nick gave a start. That one surprised

him. It was loud. His heart beat faster. Nick waved blindly, feeling for the chain to an old bare bulb on the ceiling. Found it, and pulled. Yes, it worked. Light.

Nick took a deep breath. The noise had stopped. He looked around. Off to the side, old furniture and boxes were stacked on wooden pallets. There was the boiler, the washer and dryer. A sink.

Drip, drip, drip.

Nick crossed the room to tighten the faucet. He gripped and turned with all his might. *Drip . . . drip.* There, fixed.

Then Nick glanced into the sink. He blinked, unsure of what he was seeing. Could it be? How was it possible?

The drops of water had settled into the sink in a strange pattern. There were

dry spots, and there were wet spots. Mostly, it was wet.

But the dry spots formed the shapes of letters.

It was a message for Nick.

It read:

GET OUT.

All that night, Nick lay in bed thinking. Could this all be his imagination? He didn't think so. No, the house was trying to tell him something. Warn him about something. He couldn't explain it to anyone — definitely not his parents. But Nick knew, absolutely *knew,* that the house itself was trying to speak.

He rolled over on his bed and looked at the wall. It was covered with drawings he had taped there. Drawings he had made just today. Dozens of them.

Every one was different, but the same.

A house.

On fire.

Nick heard the shower go on upstairs. He didn't think anything of it. But a few minutes later, he heard his parents talking in the dining room. The furniture was covered with drop cloths. There were paint cans and brushes sprawled on the floor.

Nick saw that his mother's hair was not wet.

Neither was his father's.

So who turned on the shower?

Nick cautiously climbed the stairs. He held tight to the railing, for stairs now made him uneasy. He crept toward the bathroom. Yes, water, he heard it now. The shower was running.

When he opened the door, the room was filled with smoke. No, not smoke. Steam. Hot steam. So thick it was hard to see. Nick reached into the shower and turned off the hot water. Slowly, the steam seeped out of the room through the open door.

The mirror was fogged up. But gradually it returned to normal. Except for four letters.

At first, Nick didn't understand it. Because the letters in the mirror were backward. The message read:

ERIF.

That night Nick tried to sleep with both the radio and the light on. He lay awake for a long, long time. Finally, he turned the radio off, rolled over, and slept a fitful sleep.

He was awakened in the middle of the night.

By the radio. It was on. Somehow it had turned itself back on.

Nick listened to it vaguely, groggy and still half-asleep. Then his eyes widened. He became alert. The radio wasn't playing music.

It was a voice. A mechanical voice, like a robot or an automated computer. The kind of voice a machine would make. If, that is, a machine could talk.

The radio, plugged into the house, said two words.

Over and over.

"Save yourself . . . save yourself . . . save yourself."

*　　*　　*

Nick stood beside his parents' bed.

"Nicholas?" his mother said in a hoarse voice. "What's the matter? You're trembling."

She snapped on the light. Felt his forehead, held his hands in hers.

"You are burning up," she said.

His father sat up. "What's wrong?"

"We have to go now," Nick told them.

"What? I don't understand. . . ." his mother said.

"All of us," Nick insisted. "We have to leave this house right now."

It took some doing. But Nick wouldn't give in. He begged and pleaded. And he would not take no for an answer.

Finally, unhappily, the entire

family — baby Lucy, his mother, his father, and Nick — pulled out of the driveway in the middle of the night. They went to the hospital. Supposedly because Nick's fever was raging out of control.

"One hundred and four degrees," his mother had said, alarmed. "He's on fire."

In the waiting room, strangely empty in the middle of the night, the Golubs' cell phone rang. Nick's father frowned, walked to the other side of the room, and answered it.

After a few moments, he sat heavily back in his chair.

"Honey, what is it?" asked Nick's mother.

Nick's father turned to his family.

His face was white. "My God," he whispered. "That was the Barbos across the street. They were scared to death."

Nick squeezed his mother's hand.

He saw that his father was staring at him. "Our house," Nick's father said, "just burned to the ground."

"What?" Nick said.

Nick's father held the phone out in his hand. "The Barbos were afraid that we were inside. So they called," he explained.

Silence filled the room the way air fills a swimmer's lungs. There was no room for anything else.

"They said there was an explosion in the boiler room," Nick's father continued. He spoke flatly, without expression. Stunned. "They said the house was an inferno within seconds. If anyone had been home, no one would have gotten out alive."

His mother sobbed. His father sat beside his son. Put a hand on his shoulder. "Nick," his father said. "Tell me, son. How did you know?"

A FRIEND
IN NEED

"Hello," Mrs. Monroe said upon opening the door. "You must be Miranda. Right on time. Please come in." She extended her right hand in greeting.

For Miranda Givens, age fifteen, it was an awkward moment. Because she had a piece of chewing gum in her hand. A well-chewed piece of gum, in fact. After ringing the bell, Miranda had decided that it would look bad for a new babysitter to arrive with gum in her mouth. So Miranda took it out. But just as she searched for a place to toss the gum, Mrs. Monroe opened the door.

"Er, um . . ." Miranda hesitated. Mrs. Monroe's hand hovered in front of her, beckoning. "I, uh, wow, you look gorgeous," Miranda finally said. She shoved the gum into the back pocket of her jeans. A mistake, Miranda immediately realized, but at least now she could shake the hand of her new employer.

Mrs. Monroe whisked away from the door, clasping a pearl necklace as she walked. She wore an evening gown that perfectly matched her ruby-red lipstick. She was all dressed up with somewhere to go.

Miranda followed Mrs. Monroe into a spacious back room with a couch, a computer, and a massive television set. "I'm happy to meet you," Mrs. Monroe began. "You have no idea how difficult it's been for us to get a sitter. All of the ones we've used seem to get new boyfriends, or join teams, or what have you."

Miranda nodded, since that seemed like the right thing to do. All the while she was thinking, *I bet these rich people have good snack food.*

The lovely, tanned, gym-toned Mrs. Monroe fixed Miranda with a gaze. "You don't have a boyfriend, do you?"

"Ummmm —" Miranda shook her head.

Mrs. Monroe smiled, relieved. "Well, don't get one — they are nothing but trouble," she said with a laugh.

49

Ba-thump, ba-thump, ba-thump.

"Ah, here comes my daughter now," Mrs. Monroe announced.

A dark-haired, dark-eyed little mouse of a five-year-old girl entered the room. She was dragging a broomstick behind her. Her hair was flat and lifeless, her skin white. She did not smile.

"Ava," Mrs. Monroe said sharply, "I've asked you not to bang that stick on the stairs."

Ava looked at the ground. "It was Jimmyjimjim," she said.

Mrs. Monroe cast a sideways glance at Miranda. "Ava has an imaginary friend," she explained.

"His name is Jimmyjimjim," Ava said. She looked toward Miranda, but not directly at her. Her gaze seemed to settle somewhere above Miranda's left shoulder. It gave Miranda an uneasy feeling, but she smiled and introduced herself anyway.

"My name is Miranda," the new babysitter said.

Ava wiggled a finger inside her nose in response.

"Well, we must be off to the charity gala," Mrs. Monroe announced. "I've left instructions on the kitchen table. Will ten dollars an hour suit you?"

"Why, um, yes," Miranda replied. Ten dollars an hour! It was three dollars more than she got from the Sweeneys, and they had four lousy kids.

Mr. Monroe appeared. He said hello to Miranda, gave Ava a distracted, half-hearted hug, and hustled out the door behind his wife.

Miranda smiled at Ava. "I guess it's just the two of us," she said.

"Three."

"Three?"

"Jimmyjimjim," Ava reminded her.

What an odd child, Miranda thought. "Does he talk?" Miranda asked.

"He won't talk to you," Ava said.

"Can you tell me what he looks like?" Miranda asked.

"Jimmyjimjim has blue eyes and blond hair," Ava answered.

"Hmmm," Miranda said. "Anything else?"

"He has no mommy and no daddy. Just me," Ava said.

"What else?"

"He's a little bit mean," Ava confided in a whisper.

"Oh?"

"Yes," Ava said. "He does bad things." She stared blankly at Miranda's knees. "Jimmyjimjim hates babysitters."

"I see," Miranda said, suddenly uncomfortable. "*Hate* isn't a very nice word."

"No, it isn't," Ava replied. "But Jimmyjimjim isn't often nice."

Miranda began to wonder about the food in the kitchen. To do a thorough search, she'd need to keep Ava busy. This was Saturday night. A most excellent TV night. "Don't you have other friends?" she idly asked Ava.

"No. Just Jimmyjimjim."

"No one else?"

Ava picked at her plain black dress. That was her answer.

"I like that name, Jimmyjimjim," Miranda said. "It's funny."

Ava laughed once without smiling, in a wicked burst, "HA!" Then her face went blank again. "FUNNY!" she screamed. Then the little girl with the imaginary friend turned and walked out of the room, dragging the broomstick behind her.

"Bye," Miranda called out. "I'll be here if you need anything."

Ba-thump, ba-thump, ba-thump.

Little Ava and Jimmyjimjim went upstairs.

Miranda grabbed a *TV Guide* off the coffee table. She headed into the kitchen. *Rich people,* she thought, *have the best junk food.*

About half an hour later, Miranda was seated on the couch watching television. She had a bowl of popcorn on her lap. A package of Twizzlers at her side. And a can of cherry soda on the table.

Life was good.

Ava suddenly appeared beside her.

"Oh my God!" Miranda exclaimed. "You scared me!"

Ava didn't say anything. Finally she leaned toward the sitter and whispered, "Jimmyjimjim did a bad thing."

Miranda followed Ava to the upstairs bathroom. "It's sticky," Ava warned her.

Miranda looked at the floor. "Is that . . . jelly?"

Ava nodded. "Grape."

"Ava, go to your room," Miranda scolded.

Ava said flatly, "Jimmyjimjim did it."

"Oh, right, your imaginary friend," scoffed Miranda. Grape jelly was smeared all over the tiles, faucets, counter, and mirror. "I don't think this is funny," Miranda fumed. "Go downstairs. You can watch television. Just stay out of my face while I clean this mess."

Ava nodded. It was Jimmyjimjim's fault. He didn't like babysitters. Not the least little bit. She paused in the hallway. "You won't tell, will you?" Ava asked.

Miranda grabbed cleaning supplies from beneath the sink. "We'll see," she said. "I'm sorry that I yelled. But please, go downstairs while I clean this up."

"Can Jimmyjimjim come, too?" Ava asked.

"Whatever."

Ava watched Miranda for a few long moments. She confided, "He can be so awful sometimes, that Jimmyjimjim."

And she drifted downstairs.

Ba-thump, ba-thump, ba-thump.

Miranda was not in a good mood when she came downstairs fifteen minutes later. Her mood was about to get a lot worse. "Where's my iPod?" she asked.

"Was it small and white, about this big?" Ava asked, holding her fingers a few inches apart.

Miranda nodded.

Ava frowned. "Jimmyjimjim was playing with it in the bathroom. I heard a splash." She turned back to the television and put a handful of popcorn into her mouth.

Naturally Miranda flipped out. This strange little girl was too much. Ava was pushing her over the edge.

Miranda raced into the bathroom. She found her iPod — in the toilet!

"Ava!" she screamed.

"It wasn't me," Ava replied flatly. "It was Jimmyjimjim."

"Where's Jimmyjimjim now?!" Miranda demanded.

Ava pointed a finger toward the ceiling. "Playing in my room," she said. "Jimmyjimjim doesn't watch girly shows."

Miranda glanced at the television. Ava had switched channels. She was watching a rerun of *Full House*. One of the Olsen twins was saying something unbearably adorable to Joey or Jesse, one of those guys.

"He's in your room?" Miranda asked again.

Ava nodded.

"Good, I'm going to lock him in," Miranda threatened. "And then you and I are going to have a talk."

Miranda stormed upstairs.

"I wouldn't do that," Ava warned.

Moments later, Miranda returned. "I locked the door," she announced. "It's just you and me."

Ava frowned. "Jimmyjimjim won't be happy."

Miranda took a sip of cherry soda. The can was empty. Ava had finished it.

"How long have you and Jimmyjimjim been friends?" Miranda asked.

"A long time. He's dead, you know. Jimmyjimjim got hit by a car" — Ava pointed toward the front door — "out there on the street."

Miranda blinked. "Yes, yes, I think I remember," she said. "It was about four or five years ago. A boy on a bicycle. He got hit by a car."

"And he died," Ava said. "Jimmyjimjim."

Miranda leaned back in her chair, speechless.

"He is my friend now," Ava told Miranda. "But he doesn't like baby-sitters."

Miranda nodded.

Crash, boom.

A series of deafening noises came from upstairs.

Miranda jumped to her feet, startled.

Ava sat, perfectly still.

"What was that?" Miranda exclaimed.

Ava shrugged. "You know, silly," she replied.

Miranda looked toward the ceiling. More noises, crashing sounds came from upstairs. "Jimmyjimjim," she murmured.

Ava blinked her big brown eyes. Very slowly. Closed. Opened. One time. Blink.

Ba-thump, ba-thump, ba-thump.

"He's coming down the stairs," Ava noted. She smiled, for the first time that night, wickedly.

Miranda didn't even say good-bye. She just ran out the door, down the street, all the way home.

It was as if, Ava mused, she had seen a ghost.

With a shrug, Ava returned to the television. Those Olsen twins were awfully funny. Much nicer than that horrid babysitter, Miranda. She was just like the others. Not nearly as nice as her mommy and her daddy.

When the Monroes arrived home later that night, they found Ava curled up asleep on the couch. All the lights were on. There was no sitter in sight. The upstairs bedroom was a shambles, full of broken furniture and smashed glass.

It would be a long, long while before they went out again. For, you see, it's so awfully hard to find a good sitter.

As for Ava, she knew who to thank. Jimmyjimjim was always there for Ava when she needed a friend. Because to be honest, Ava didn't like babysitters, either. It was nicer when Mom and Dad stayed home. At least that's what Ava thought.

And Jimmyjimjim agreed.

HOME, SWEET HORROR

Ruby opened her eyes. She liked the sound they made, *click*, when she blinked. She lay on her back and stared at the top of her canopy bed. The blankets were warm and soft and as blue as a robin's egg. Ruby believed that she could lie for days and days without moving a muscle. How quiet and how lovely!

Ruby thought, *So this is my new home*. The house was silent. Ruby looked around at her bedroom. For fun, she tried looking at the room without turning her head. Instead Ruby rolled her eyes around in their sockets and stole sideways glances from wall to wall. Everything was beautiful. Everything, Ruby noted with satisfaction, was just so.

This will do just fine, she decided.

The dresser was mahogany, a brownish-red color, and it appeared to Ruby that the drawers really worked. A free-standing closet, called an armoire, stood against the opposite wall. One door of the armoire was ajar. Ruby counted five white coat hangers all in a row, neat and tidy. On the matching mahogany night table was a blue hurricane lamp and the most precious little box of tissues that Ruby had ever seen.

But goodness, one can't lie about forever! So Ruby sat up. She swung her legs off the bed. Oh, dear, they were stiff. Maybe they would loosen up after a while. Ruby decided to explore.

The house was more perfect than she had hoped. Every room had been put together with loving care. Persian rugs in the living room, bright wallpaper, candlesticks on the mantelpiece, and so much more. Every detail made it look as if — why yes, that was it! — as if it were ordered from a catalog. Ruby's favorite item was a birdcage on a stand. Strange, though. There was no bird to be found.

"Must have flown the coop," Ruby said to herself, giggling softly.

She heard the clinking of cups and saucers coming from the kitchen. Ruby's heart fell silent. *My new parents*, Ruby mused. She ran a hand through her thick golden curls, tried to smile, and walked stiff-legged into the kitchen.

An old man and an old woman sat at the table. They stared absently at each other. There was a lovely teapot, cups, and even a dainty plate of cookies laid out on the table. However, the two old folks did not turn to look at Ruby. Not even a glance.

Neither of them touched their tea. Ruby looked around. The floor and walls were a buttery yellow. A happy color. And the fridge, oven, and sink were all so . . . What was the word? . . . So realistic.

"What are you doing out of your room?" the old woman snarled.

"Excuse me?" Ruby replied.

The old man coughed. "You are not supposed to be here," he said in a gruff voice. "What if She were to find you? What would happen then? Tell me — what would happen then?"

Ruby did not know how to answer. The questions were so impolite. "Well, surely . . ." she began.

"Pish and tosh," the old woman grumbled. "I see that you're a fancy one. Such a pretty, pretty dress. Must have cost an arm and a leg," she hissed. There was nothing pleasant about the way the old woman spoke to Ruby. Nothing at all.

"I'm quite sure I don't understand," Ruby said.

The old man chuckled at that. "You will," he said grimly. "You will understand soon enough."

Bitter laughter came from the old woman's lips.

Ruby felt uneasy. Something wasn't right. "Is it just us?" she asked. "Are we all alone?"

"Not alone," the old woman mumbled.

"I'm sure She'll *love* you," the old man said.

"So pretty," the old woman said. "So nicely put together. Aren't you just the latest thing? She'll brush your hair and tuck you into bed each night, I'll bet."

The old man nodded.

"For a time," the old woman added.

Scritch, scratch.

A short gasp came from the woman. The man froze. "Hide," the old man whispered to Ruby. "The beast comes."

An unseen door creaked loudly. The old couple sat frozen in fear. Ruby darted into the next room and ducked behind a red velvet sofa. She strained to listen. She heard the near-silent steps of a creature on padded paws. *Click*, Ruby closed her eyes in fright. *Click*, she opened them again.

That's when Ruby realized that one wall of the room was missing. Really, there was no other way to describe it. The wall, or where there should have been a wall, was not there. Instead there was . . . nothing. No "thing" at all.

How very, very odd.

Ruby lay on her stomach and pulled

herself along the carpet. She crept to the edge of the room. And — heavens — she might as well have been at the edge of the world. Where the floor ended there was only air. A drop of some impossible distance. As if she were in a house floating on a cloud.

How could that be? Ruby wondered. *What is this place?*

And then she saw it.

The beast was much larger than dear, stiff-legged Ruby. Much, much larger.

It was all black. Four long legs and a thick round tail. Ruby gasped. The beast paused, one paw in midstep. Its head turned. It looked up and stared into Ruby's eyes.

The beast had green eyes. It licked its mouth. Long whiskers grew from its horrible face. Sharp pointed ears rose from its head. Ruby slowly crawled away, pushing herself back behind the sofa. She covered her head with her hands. And though Ruby wished to cry, no tears came.

The next few minutes were more awful than Ruby could have ever imagined. She heard noises in the kitchen. Overturned chairs. Snuffling and banging and clawing and — oh, yes — the desperate cries of the old woman.

Not a sound came from the old man.

Then it stopped. As quickly as it began.

The only sound left was the old woman's weeping.

Ruby walked into the kitchen. The table had been overturned. The old woman sat slumped against a wall. Her eyes were fixed on one spot.

The old man lay on the floor.

His arm was gone.

There were bite marks on his head and body.

Suddenly — *BOOM, BOOM, BOOM!* A thunderous noise roared like mighty waves crashing upon a rocky shore. Louder and louder it roared, closer and closer. Ruby knelt by the old man, her hand on his back.

"She comes," he groaned. "Now you will see."

"See what?" Ruby begged the old man. "What will I see?"

"The horror," he said. "The horror."

Her eyes frantically searched the room. "What is this place?" Ruby pleaded. "Where am I?"

"I'LL BE IN MY ROOM!" screamed a voice. It was terrifying. So loud, so near.

"Dinner is in five minutes," another voice called, as if from a far distance.

"OKAY!" the near voice screamed. Ruby's ears nearly burst at the sound. "I'LL BE PLAYING WITH MY DOLLHOUSE," the voice called out.

Ruby closed her eyes. *Click*. She stood on stiff legs. She dared not breathe. *Dollhouse,* Ruby thought. *At last I understand.*

A giant, hideous, most disgusting face hovered close to Ruby. The nose was monstrous, with horrid nostrils and fleshy knobs of skin. The creature's thick red lips curled upward, revealing large white teeth. "However did you get here?" the girl said. "Oh, my. Has my little kitten been sneaking around in my room again? Poor Papa, you lost an arm!"

A giant hand reached for Ruby.

Its fingers wrapped tightly around her waist. Squeezing her, lifting her, taking her away.

Poor Ruby. Such a doll. She could not even scream. And though she wanted to cry, no tears came.